Sheltie Saves the Day

Peter Clover

PUFFIN BOOKS

PUFFIN BOOKS

Published by the Penguin Group
Penguin Books Ltd, 80 Strand, London WC2R 0RL, England
Penguin Putnam Inc., 375 Hudson Street, New York, New York 10014, USA
Penguin Books Australia Ltd, Ringwood, Victoria, Australia
Penguin Books Canada Ltd, 10 Alcorn Avenue, Toronto, Ontario, Canada M4V 3B2
Penguin Books India (P) Ltd, 11 Community Centre, Panchsheel Park, New Delhi – 110 017, India
Penguin Books (NZ) Ltd, Cnr Rosedale and Airborne Roads, Albany, Auckland, New Zealand
Penguin Books (South Africa) (Pty) Ltd, 24 Sturdee Avenue, Rosebank 2196 South Africa

Penguin Books Ltd, Registered Offices: 80 Strand, London WC2R 0RL, England

www.penguin.com

Penguin Books Ltd, Registered Offices: Harmondsworth, Middlesex, England

First published 1996
15 17 19 20 18 16 14

Created by Working Partners Ltd, London W6 0HE

The moral right of the author/illustrator has been asserted

Filmset in 14/20 Palatino

Made and printed in England by Clays Ltd, St Ives plc

British Library Cataloguing in Publication Data
A CIP catalogue record for this book is available from the British Library

ISBN 0–140–38132–5

Chapter One

That morning, Emma's mum and dad had decided to paint the wooden gate at the front of the cottage. Mum was busy with the sandpaper, rubbing the wooden posts smooth. Dad was stirring the paint and keeping an eye on little Joshua at the same time. Joshua kept trying to dip his fingers into the creamy white goo.

All three suddenly looked up

together, as Emma came racing up the lane on Sheltie, her little Shetland pony.

Dad smiled. 'Here comes the Lone Ranger,' he said. Mum laughed and Joshua jumped up and down, clapping his hands together. He very nearly kicked the pot of paint over.

Joshua always got excited when he saw Emma riding Sheltie. He thought Sheltie was a racehorse. And if Emma ever took Sheltie over a jump, Joshua's eyes would grow wide like saucers.

Emma and Sheltie came to a halt with a clatter of hooves on the gravel path. Mum jumped back, startled.

'Did you forget to put the brakes on, Emma?' said Mum.

Dad had never seen her in such a hurry before. Emma's face was all red.

She looked very angry and upset. She jumped out of the saddle and landed with a thud.

'Whatever is wrong?' asked Dad.

'It's Horseshoe Pond, Dad. It's awful,' said Emma.

'Horseshoe Pond isn't awful at all, Emma,' said Mum. 'It's beautiful.'

'I know,' said Emma. 'Horseshoe Pond *is* beautiful. That's why it's awful what they're going to do to it.'

'Who's *they*?' asked Mum. 'And what are *they* going to do?'

Sheltie began to snort and blow. He shook his long shaggy mane.

'Sheltie thinks it's awful too,' said Emma. 'Men are coming to fill in Horseshoe Pond. They're going to pull down all the trees and flatten Prickly

3

Thicket to make a rotten caravan park! It's awful, Mum.'

'Surely not,' said Dad. 'Horseshoe Pond is on Mr Brown's farm. Mr Brown would never let a thing like that happen. A caravan park. I don't think so, Emma.'

'But it's true, isn't it, Sheltie?' said Emma.

Sheltie scraped at the gravel with his hoof. He always did that when he was trying to tell Emma something.

'I overheard Mrs Jenkins talking to the gardener. Mrs Jenkins said it was the worst news she had ever heard. And that she'd got it straight from the horse's mouth. But I don't know which horse it was that told her.'

Although it was a serious matter,

Mum smiled and said, 'That's only a saying, Emma. Horses don't really talk.'

'Well, Sheltie does,' said Emma. 'I understand everything he says. Don't I, Sheltie?'

Sheltie's eyes twinkled beneath his long mane. He nodded his head three times.

'See?' Emma said brightly. 'And Sheltie understands every word I say too. Don't you, Sheltie?'

The pony nodded again.

Joshua gurgled and squealed with laughter.

'Anyway,' said Emma. 'Sheltie isn't a horse. He's a Shetland pony. A very special Shetland pony.'

Emma threw her arms around Sheltie's neck and gave the little pony a big hug. Then she gave him one of his favourite peppermints. Sheltie loved peppermints.

Emma's dad went inside the cottage to telephone Mr Brown. He was going to ask the farmer if Emma's story was true.

Five minutes later when Dad came out again, his face looked grim.

'It's true, I'm afraid,' said Dad. 'Every word of it.'

Mr Brown was in trouble. Last year his tractor broke down and he was forced to borrow money to buy a new one.

This year he needed a new combine harvester. Without it he wouldn't be able to harvest his cornfields in the autumn.

Mr Brown needed money. And the only way he could get it was to sell off some of his land.

Two men were already interested in buying Horseshoe Pond and the big meadow. A little thicket of prickly holly bushes grew there too, and it was all going to be taken away.

'I don't think there's anything anyone

can do,' said Dad. Emma lowered her
head and led Sheltie back to his
paddock. She felt very sad.

Chapter Two

Horseshoe Pond was one of Emma's favourite places. The pond was in the shape of a horseshoe and where its two ends almost met and touched, there was a little hump of grass like an island. Emma liked to sit there and look out across the pond to the rolling hills, while Sheltie nibbled at the long grass.

There was a big sycamore tree which

grew on the island. Emma would sit beneath it and listen to the birds as she watched the fish and the dragonflies.

Emma would pretend that she was a princess or sometimes a pirate queen and that the island was her castle or pirate ship. And all the land as far as she could see belonged to her.

Emma couldn't imagine what Little Applewood would be like with no Horseshoe Pond and no magical island.

The next day, two men came in a jeep with shovels and spades. They put up a tent in Mr Brown's meadow and set up camp.

When Emma and Sheltie came trotting along, the two men were already busy at work. They were measuring things with a long tape and

marking areas off all around the
meadow with sticks and flags.

When the two men saw Emma and
Sheltie, they both stopped and looked
up. One of the men had black hair and
a beard. The other man's hair was
bright red and curly. Emma didn't like
the look of them. Neither did Sheltie.

When Emma said 'Good morning',
the two men just stared. The man with
the beard spoke.

'And where do you think you're
going, miss?'

'Horseshoe Pond,' said Emma. 'I
always go there and sit under the tree.'

'Well, not any more you don't,' said
the man. 'You're not to come anywhere
near here.'

Sheltie gave a loud blow from his

nostrils. Emma didn't like the way the
man spoke. Then she heard a voice
behind her.

'Emma can come here as often as she
likes.' It was Mr Brown. He ruffled
Sheltie's long mane as he spoke. 'Don't
you take any notice, Emma. The
meadow hasn't been sold yet. It still

belongs to me. I've only given these men permission to take measurements and make some tests before the sale goes through. In the mean time you can come here whenever you want.'

Mr Brown gave the two men a stern, no-nonsense look. They grumbled under their breath and stomped off over to their jeep.

Mr Brown turned and spoke to Emma. His voice was kind and filled with sadness.

'You can sit by the pond as long as you wish, Emma,' he said. 'Those men won't bother you.'

Emma gave a weak smile, then rode Sheltie over to the pond and jumped down from the saddle. Sheltie bent his head and nibbled on the fresh green shoots which grew there. Emma sat on the little island and watched Mr Brown walk back to the farm.

Emma didn't want to stay there for long because the two men kept looking over at her. But she felt that she should sit there for a little while because Mr Brown had been so kind.

Chapter Three

A few minutes later, the man with red hair came walking across the meadow. Emma's heart was beating fast.

'Hello,' said the man. He sounded friendly. 'I'm sorry if my friend was rude before, only we have a lot of work to do and we can't get on with it if there are too many people around.'

Emma didn't say anything. She

wished Mr Brown would come back. Sheltie stopped munching grass and looked up. His eyes shone, bright and alert. Emma noticed that the man was holding a piece of paper. The paper looked old and worn at the edges.

'What are you measuring?' asked Emma.

'Um, we're measuring for the drains,' said the man very quickly.

'And do you really have to fill in the pond?' asked Emma.

'Of course,' said the man. 'We can get at least three caravans where that pond is.'

Emma looked up through the leaves of the tree.

'Will you keep the tree?' asked Emma.

The man looked at the big sycamore

as though he had just seen it for the
first time.

'It's only an old tree,' said the man.
He waved the piece of paper towards
Prickly Thicket. 'All those will be
coming down too,' he said.

Suddenly, without warning, Sheltie
lurched forward and snatched the piece
of paper out of the man's hand. The
man jumped, but Sheltie was very

quick and ran off across the meadow with the piece of paper in his mouth.

The man was very angry and yelled at Sheltie as he galloped away. Emma leapt to her feet.

'Sheltie, come back!' called Emma. But Sheltie took no notice. He was off, running back to his paddock as fast as he could.

The other man saw what had happened. He dropped the spade he was holding and tried to cut Sheltie off at the gate. But Sheltie reached the gate first and charged up the lane on his short little legs. The two men followed, huffing and puffing, with Emma running close behind.

When Sheltie reached the paddock, he flew into his little shelter at the end of the field. The two men were making a lot of noise. They were hollering and shouting so loudly that Dad came out of the cottage to see what all the fuss was about.

The two men were in the paddock, peering into Sheltie's field shelter. They were both shaking with rage as they watched a tiny corner of the paper disappear into Sheltie's mouth. With one gulp and a swallow it was gone.

'Oh, Sheltie. You naughty boy,' said Emma. But deep down inside, Emma was pleased. She didn't like the two men one little bit.

'What is going on?' asked Dad. The man with the black beard pointed to Sheltie. He jabbed at the air with his finger.

'That *thing* has eaten our document!'

Dad told the man to calm down and stop shouting. Mum had come out of the cottage now and came over to see what was going on. She held Emma's hand.

'He didn't mean to, honest,' said Emma. 'Sheltie's never done anything like that before. He's ever so sorry.'

Just then, PC Green, the village

policeman, came riding up the lane on his bicycle. He heard all the shouting and rode straight into the paddock.

When the two men saw the policeman they went very quiet.

'What seems to be the trouble?' said PC Green.

Emma told the policeman what Sheltie had done. She said that Sheltie was very sorry.

The policeman said that under the circumstances there was nothing that could be done and sent the two men away.

Chapter Four

That evening, when Mum came
upstairs to say goodnight to Emma,
Emma was lying in bed looking up at
the pictures on her bedroom wall.
They were pictures of Horseshoe
Pond and the big sycamore tree which
grew there. Emma had drawn them
herself.

'I think Sheltie knows that those men
are going to fill in the pond,' said

Emma. 'That's why he ate their silly piece of paper.'

Mum thought that perhaps Emma was right. She said goodnight and switched off the light.

All night long, Emma tossed and turned in her bed. She kept thinking of Horseshoe Pond and the new caravan park. She couldn't sleep a wink.

It was very late and dark when Emma heard Sheltie outside in his paddock. He was making funny whinnying noises. Emma got out of bed and looked out of the window.

In the moonlight she could see Sheltie standing by the fence. Emma looked beyond the paddock and out towards the meadow and Horseshoe Pond. In the daytime she could see the sycamore tree and just make out the water shimmering in the little pond. In the darkness Emma couldn't see a thing, but she looked all the same.

What is that? she thought. She looked hard. Emma could see a strange light moving around in the meadow. She stood at the window and watched the light in the meadow moving slowly to and fro.

Sheltie was still making funny noises and now he was pawing at the ground. Emma knew that Sheltie wanted to show her something. Emma decided to go and take a look. If she was quiet, then no one would ever know.

Emma got dressed and tiptoed downstairs. She unlocked the kitchen door and crept down the garden path.

When Sheltie saw her he gave a noisy
blow and tossed his head.

'Shh, Sheltie!' Emma whispered as
she unlocked the gate and went into
the paddock.

Sheltie gave a little sneeze and urged
Emma to follow him across to the far
side of the field where a tall hedge
separated the paddock from Mr
Brown's meadow. The night was clear
and warm. Emma looked up at the
moon and stars twinkling in the sky.
The moonlight made the hedge and all
the grass shine silver.

Emma climbed up on to the bank
using the twisted roots like a ladder.
She stood with one foot on Sheltie's
back to steady herself.

'Stand still, Sheltie,' said Emma.

'And stop fidgeting!'

Emma peered over the top of the hedge into the meadow. She could clearly see that it was the two men walking about. One of the men was shining a torch on the ground. The other man was holding a funny kind of stick. On the end of the stick close to the ground was a flat, round disc. It looked like a big frying pan with a very long handle.

The man was passing the frying pan slowly over the grass. A little light on the handle was flashing as he walked along. As Emma's eyes got used to the dark, she could see that the man with the frying pan was wearing headphones.

Every now and again the man stopped, and the other one marked the spot with a small yellow peg.

What are they doing? thought Emma. *And why are they doing it in the middle of the night*?

Whatever it was, she guessed it must be something secret. Something they didn't want Mr Brown or anyone to know about.

The next morning, Emma woke bright and early. She had a bowl of cereal for

breakfast, then went outside to feed
Sheltie. One scoop of pony mix plus
one tiny handful for luck.

Normally, Sheltie would push his
nose into the feeding manger before
Emma had finished scooping. But
today he just stood there and watched.
He was blowing and snorting and
stamping the ground.

'What is it, Sheltie?'

Emma was puzzled. Was he trying to
tell her something?

Sheltie began scraping at the floor.
As he pushed the hay aside, Emma
noticed a piece of paper lying on the
floor. It was the same paper that he had
snatched from the two men the day
before.

Sheltie hadn't eaten it after all! He

had been pretending and had only bitten off and swallowed one tiny corner.

Emma picked up the paper and held it in both hands. It was a map. An old drawing of Little Applewood. She recognized the meadow from the horseshoe shape of the pond. The sycamore tree and the thicket of shrubs and bushes were clearly marked.

Emma found her cottage on the map and traced her finger along the lane

down to the meadow. The farm was also marked and so was Fox Hall Manor. There were also lots of crosses drawn all over the paper. Emma counted them. There were at least twenty.

Emma turned the map over. On the back of the paper, printed at the very top in fine, fancy letters was a name and address. *Major Armstrong, Fox Hall Manor, Little Applewood, Chittlewink.* The map was scribbled on the back of old notepaper from the manor house.

Emma didn't know what to do. She thought it best to show Mum and Dad straight away. But Dad had already gone off to work, and Mum was busy in the kitchen, making posters for the local police force charity dinner.

Little Joshua sat at the table watching. Mum was trying to keep him out of the paint pots. His hands were already covered with sticky glue.

'Oh, Emma,' said Mum. 'Would you be an angel and take these cakes down the lane to Mr Crock for me? They're to say thank you for all those carrots he gave me the other day.' Six fairy cakes were packed into a little red tin on the table.

Emma put the map in the pocket of her jeans and took the cakes. She decided to show Mum the map later, when she wasn't so busy.

Chapter Five

Mr Crock was in his vegetable garden planting out turnips. Sheltie stuck his nose over the stone wall and blew a raspberry. When Mr Crock looked up and saw that it was Sheltie, he smiled.

'Hello, Emma,' he said. They had become good friends, and Mr Crock wasn't half as grumpy as he used to be. He thanked Emma for the cakes and asked if she would like one with a glass of homemade lemonade.

Emma followed Mr Crock through into the kitchen and watched him pour two drinks from a big jug. Sheltie looked in through the kitchen window. Emma had made him promise to be on his best behaviour.

As Emma ate her cake and drank her lemonade, she decided to show Mr Crock the map, and tell him all about the two men and their funny frying pan.

Mr Crock listened carefully to every word. Then he held the map and studied both sides of the paper.

'I think I know just what this is, Emma,' he said. 'Many years ago, before the old Major died, he started to worry that robbers might steal his valuables. So one day, the silly old fool gathered together all his treasures and took them out and buried them! He buried his treasure in some secret place, then forgot where he'd buried it.

'His family were very upset and searched everywhere, for part of the treasure that Major Armstrong had buried was the family collection of gold coins.

'There was a story that he'd drawn a map, but he couldn't remember where he'd put that either. No one ever found the map and the treasure was lost. The Major must have hidden the map in an old book or something.

'You know what I think this is, Emma? Major Armstrong's lost treasure map.'

'And those two men must have found it and are looking for the old Major's treasure!' said Emma.

Mr Crock told Emma that the men's funny frying pan was probably a metal detector.

'People use them to find metal objects such as coins buried beneath the ground.'

'What are we going to do?' asked Emma. 'Should we tell the police?'

Mr Crock thought hard for a moment. 'Perhaps it would be best for now if we didn't tell anyone, Emma. After all, those men haven't really done anything wrong. And we can't prove that they are looking for Major Armstrong's treasure, can we?'

'But if they do find it, I bet they'll use

the money to fill in Horseshoe Pond
and build their rotten caravan park,'
said Emma.

'Well, you'll just have to find it first,'
said Mr Crock. 'Why don't you take a
walk up to Horseshoe Pond and see
what those two men are up to?'

When they went back outside,
Sheltie was standing with his head in
an apple tree, helping himself.

'Sheltie, you naughty boy!' said Emma.

'It's all right, Emma,' said Mr Crock. 'There are plenty of apples in that old tree. I don't suppose I'll miss one or two. But they're not very ripe yet. I hope Sheltie doesn't mind!'

Sheltie was full of mischief and pulled another apple from a branch of the tree.

'No, I don't think he minds at all,' said Emma.

Chapter Six

Emma rode Sheltie back down the lane to Mr Brown's meadow. When they got to Horseshoe Pond there was no sign of the two men, but there were small holes dug all over the meadow next to the little yellow pegs.

Emma glanced at her wristwatch. It was ten o'clock.

'They must still be asleep in their tent, Sheltie,' she said. 'I expect they're very tired if they've been up all night digging these holes.'

Sheltie looked at the holes and nodded. Then Emma had an idea.

'We'll come back nice and early tomorrow, Sheltie. And play a trick.' Emma chuckled to herself as they walked away.

In the afternoon, Emma gave Sheltie's coat a good brush. As she untangled all the knots in his long mane, Emma thought about Major Armstrong and his treasure. *Fancy not remembering where he'd buried it*, thought Emma. What a silly man he was!

Emma thought hard. She wondered where *she* would bury a secret treasure.

'I think I would bury it in a place where no one could see me digging,' she told Sheltie. 'Not out in an open meadow.'

Sheltie cocked his head to one side. He was listening carefully to every word that Emma said. Emma began to comb Sheltie's long tail. It was so long it almost touched the ground.

'I would bury it somewhere hidden away. Somewhere where people would never go.'

Then Emma thought of just the place. 'I know, Sheltie!'

The little pony's ears pricked up.

'I would bury it under the biggest holly bush in Prickly Thicket. No one would think of looking for it there.'

Sheltie nodded and sneezed. He thought Prickly Thicket would be the perfect place too.

The more that Emma thought about where she would bury the treasure, the more she wanted to go and take a look, just to see if old Major Armstrong himself had thought of that very same spot.

Emma decided to take Sheltie out for a ride. Prickly Thicket seemed just the place.

Emma knew that the men would be working in the meadow. But she thought that if she kept to the far side of the field, she could nip into Prickly Thicket without being seen.

It was three o'clock when Emma rode Sheltie along by the back fence of the meadow. The two men were there, just as Emma expected. They were still poking around with sticks and digging little holes where the yellow pegs were.

Emma rode Sheltie over as close to Prickly Thicket as she dared, then jumped down from the saddle and led the way into the bushes.

Sheltie stood on guard as Emma went to explore. But he quickly found a young shrub near by with green, tender leaves and was soon munching his way through it.

Emma picked up a long stick. There were lots of small trees and shrubs growing there as well as prickly holly bushes. Emma used the stick to brush the scratchy branches aside. There were stinging nettles too, so Emma had to be very careful. She made her way through the thicket to a big holly bush which she knew was there.

Emma stood before the big holly bush. It was covered with millions of prickly leaves and grew in a big round ball.

That's where I would bury the treasure! thought Emma. It would be very difficult for anyone trying to dig it up without getting scratched to pieces.

She walked around the bush then crouched down on the grass and peered beneath the lowest branches. There was a small gap on one side, like a secret opening which led into the middle of the giant bush. Emma crawled inside.

The prickly leaves pulled at her hair and caught on her sweatshirt. Emma pushed the branches aside with the stick. Then she prodded the stick ahead of her and poked at the ground.

The stick tapped against something solid. It was a rock. A large stone right in the centre of the bush.

Emma inched her way forward. The rock was the size of a football but flatter. A white cross was painted on top of the rock. The paint was grey and flaky in parts, but Emma could see the cross quite clearly.

Suddenly, a voice from behind her made Emma jump.

'What are you doing in there?'

Chapter Seven

Emma dropped the stick and crawled backwards out of the bush. The man with ginger hair stood looking down at her with his hands resting on his hips. Emma looked up slowly. She felt her face turning red.

'Nothing!' said Emma. 'I was just looking for mushrooms.'

'Mushrooms don't grown under holly bushes!' said the man.

'Sometimes they do,' said Emma. 'They grow all over this thicket.'

'Well, you'd better look somewhere else. We don't like kids messing around when we're working, and we want to come up here in a minute.' The man turned away and walked back to the jeep.

Emma rushed over to Sheltie and jumped into the saddle. In minutes, she was racing back down the lane to tell Mr Crock all about her discovery.

The next day, Mr Crock met Emma in the paddock bright and early. He carried a trowel and a large plastic carrier bag. Emma had just finished giving Sheltie his breakfast and was filling the water trough from the rubber hose.

'Here are the things you wanted, Emma. I can't come with you. I'm too busy. But you be careful and don't go getting yourself into trouble!'

It was eight o'clock when Emma and Sheltie disappeared up the lane.

When they got to the meadow the two men were nowhere to be seen. They were both fast asleep inside their tent, just as Emma had thought they would be.

'We must be very quiet, Sheltie,' Emma whispered.

She tiptoed over to some freshly dug holes. Then she made some new ones near by. Emma reached into the carrier bag and pulled out some old tin cans. She dropped them into the holes, then shovelled the earth back in. Sheltie

helped by pressing the soil down with
his hooves.

'This will give that metal detector
something to find,' chuckled Emma.

They buried all the tin cans as
quickly as they could. Emma wondered
what the men's faces would look like

when they dug them up, thinking it
was Major Armstrong's treasure.

They tiptoed past the tent again on
the way to Prickly Thicket. Emma
could hear the two men snoring inside.
They were still fast asleep.

Emma led Sheltie to the big holly
bush and showed him the opening in
the side. Sheltie gave a loud snort and
shook his mane.

'Now, make sure that you keep
watch properly this time,' said Emma.
Then she crawled inside the bush and
ran her hand over the smooth stone
with its white cross painted on the
surface.

'Looks like we may have found
something here all right, Sheltie,' said
Emma.

Sheltie kept watch while Emma
moved the stone and began digging.

Chapter Eight

Emma had only been digging for a little while when her trowel hit something solid with a dull 'clunk'. She pushed away the earth and uncovered a large metal box. The box had two rusty handles on each side and a big lock at the front.

It was about the size of a small suitcase and very heavy. Emma was so excited.

'It's the treasure, Sheltie! We've found Major Armstrong's treasure!'

Sheltie tossed his head and gave a loud snort.

Emma tried to drag the box out of the hole but it wouldn't budge.

'Goodness knows what's in here, Sheltie. It weighs a ton.'

Just then, Emma glanced behind her through a gap in the trees and bushes towards the meadow. She saw the two men coming out of the tent. They stood there, yawning and stretching their arms.

'Oh, Sheltie! The men have woken up,' said Emma.

When Sheltie looked over, both men were rubbing their eyes. They were still very sleepy and hadn't noticed Emma and Sheltie.

'We'd better hide this box again before they see us,' said Emma. She crawled back into the bush, then re-covered the box with earth and placed the stone back on top.

Sheltie stayed well out of sight until the treasure was buried again. Then, keeping very low, Emma led Sheltie through the bushes to the far side of Prickly Thicket. They followed the fence which ran along the back of the meadow, out of sight and away. The two men didn't notice a thing.

Emma's heart was thumping as they squeezed through a gap in the fence and joined the track which led back to the lane.

When they got to the paddock

Sheltie snorted and gave a loud blow as if to say 'That was a close one!'

Emma was so excited that she could hardly breathe. She looked down and saw that her clothes were covered in mud.

Mum came out of the kitchen and went down to the paddock with little Joshua bouncing along behind. When Joshua saw Emma's muddy jeans he clapped his hands together and laughed.

'What on earth have you been up to, Emma?' said Mum. 'You're filthy.'

Emma's shoes were muddy too and she had dirt all over her face and hands.

'Picking mushrooms,' Emma said quickly. She glanced at Sheltie. 'We've been looking for mushrooms in Mr Brown's back field.'

Mum noticed that they didn't have one single mushroom between them.

'You didn't have much luck then!' she said.

'No,' said Emma. 'Perhaps we'll be luckier tomorrow.'

Mum looked puzzled.

'What are you two up to?' she said.

'Nothing,' said Emma. Then she jumped back into the saddle and trotted out into the lane. 'I'm just popping up to see Mr Crock for a minute,' Emma called over her shoulder. 'I won't be long.'

Mum watched them disappear up the lane. Then she turned to Joshua.

'I'm sure those two are up to something!'

That night, when everyone was fast asleep, Emma got out of bed and stood by the window. She looked out into the darkness over to Horseshoe Pond.

Emma could see the lights moving about in the meadow again. She smiled to herself. She imagined the two men's faces as they dug up the old tin cans.

I bet they'll be really mad, she thought.

She could see Sheltie standing by the paddock fence and blew him a goodnight kiss.

See you in the morning, Sheltie. Tomorrow is Treasure Day!

Chapter Nine

Emma was up and dressed by half past seven. She pulled on her green wellies and went downstairs.

'My goodness, Emma,' said Dad. 'You're up early.'

Dad wasn't working today. He was going to make a start on Joshua's bedroom, stripping the old wallpaper off the walls. Mum was already busy at the kitchen table finishing her posters for the charity dinner.

'Where are you off to then?' said Mum.

'Sheltie and I are taking Mr Crock mushroom picking in Mr Brown's back meadow,' said Emma. 'We have to be there early to pick the best ones.'

'Well, we'll look forward to having mushrooms on toast for our lunch, won't we, Joshua?' said Dad. 'That is, if Sheltie doesn't eat them all first.'

Moments later, Mr Crock arrived pushing a wheelbarrow. Sheltie stood with his ears pricked up and blew Mr Crock a loud raspberry.

'Cheeky monkey,' growled Mr Crock.

'Morning, Mr Crock,' Mum said as

she wandered out into the yard. She smiled when she saw the wheelbarrow.

'Do you think you might fill the whole barrow? That would keep us all in mushrooms for years!'

'I thought I might as well collect some firewood while I'm at it,' said Mr Crock. 'No sense in wasting a trip to the thicket.'

'Well, good luck,' said Mum. She stood at the back door and watched as Emma and Sheltie led Mr Crock and his wheelbarrow up the lane.

It was still and almost quiet in Mr Brown's meadow. The two men were snoring soundly inside their tent, fast asleep.

As they pushed the wheelbarrow past the tent, Emma noticed a heap of old tin cans piled up by a number of freshly dug holes. Emma and Mr Crock looked at each other and exchanged a secret wink.

'I bet they were surprised when they dug that lot up!' whispered Emma.

They wheeled the barrow into Prickly Thicket. Sheltie led the way and pushed aside all the prickly branches. His coat was very thick so he didn't feel any of the scratchy twigs and leaves.

They parked the barrow next to the big holly bush. Inside the barrow was an old blanket. Mr Crock took the blanket and laid it on the grass. Then Emma took the small trowel and crawled into the bush.

It was much easier this time. Emma pushed the stone aside and shovelled

the loose earth away. Mr Crock kept
watch through the trees, checking the
tent across the other side of the meadow.

Emma tied a rope around Sheltie and
attached the ends to one of the handles.
Then Sheltie dragged the metal box out
on to the grass.

Emma shovelled all the earth back
into the empty hole and replaced the
rock. She stood there with Sheltie and

Mr Crock looking down at the treasure chest.

'Best not to try and open it here,' said Mr Crock. 'Let's get it away safely and take it to PC Green. He'll know what to do.'

Mr Crock helped Emma to lift the box. It was very heavy, but they managed to load it into the wheelbarrow. Then Emma covered the box with the blanket.

'There, that's done,' said Mr Crock. 'Now all we have to do is get this barrow past that tent before those two sleepyheads wake up.'

Emma felt her heart sink in her chest. Her legs suddenly felt all wobbly. As she glanced over into the meadow she saw the two men standing by the tent!

Chapter Ten

The two men were both looking over towards Prickly Thicket.

'Oh no!' said Emma. 'They've seen us. They're coming over. What shall we do?'

Mr Crock began to pick up odd bits of branches and old twigs.

'Hurry, Emma. Pile as much firewood as you can into the barrow!'

They worked as fast as they could,

covering the blanket and treasure chest with dry twigs. Soon the wheelbarrow was piled high.

The two men strode into the thicket. The treasure chest and blanket were hidden from view. Well, almost.

'What are you two doing snooping around?' said the man with the black beard. He looked very angry and carried a big stick in his hand.

'We're not snooping around,' said Emma. 'We're collecting firewood. Mr Brown doesn't mind. It keeps the thicket clear and it's good wood for the burner.'

'Collecting firewood in the middle of the summer. Sounds a bit funny to me.'

'Not as funny as digging holes all over the meadow,' growled Mr Crock. 'What are you two up to anyway?'

'None of your business,' snapped the man. 'Now take that pony and that rotten old barrow out of here and be on your way. We've got important work to do!'

Emma and Mr Crock were only too happy to be on their way. Emma helped Mr Crock to lift the wheelbarrow handles and they started to push. But the barrow was very heavy and it took all of their strength to make it move.

'A bit heavy for a load of old twigs, isn't it?' said the man with the beard. 'Just what else have you got in there?'

The man with red hair glanced down at the wheelbarrow. He could see a corner of the blanket poking out at the side.

'What's this?' he said, reaching forward and grabbing the blanket. He gave it a hard tug and all the firewood fell off on to the grass. They all stood there, staring down at Major Armstrong's treasure chest.

'Well, well, well. And what have we here?' said the man with the black beard. He tapped on the metal box with his stick. 'Been doing a bit of digging on your own, have you?' he said. 'Seems like you two have found exactly what we've been looking for! Get some rope from the jeep, Red.'

Emma shouted, 'Run, Sheltie. Run!'

The man swung the stick but Sheltie was off, galloping away through the thicket.

'Hurry with that rope, Red. I'll keep these two here.'

Emma felt like crying. Tears welled in her eyes but she was determined to be brave.

The man pointed the stick at Mr Crock.

'Now you just behave yourself and keep quiet. And don't do anything stupid!'

Mr Crock stood with his hands at his sides. Emma's legs felt like jelly.

The other man came back with the rope and tied them up.

'Put them against that tree, Red,' said the man waving the stick.

Emma and Mr Crock sat beneath the tree with their hands and feet tied together.

'You won't get away with this,' said Mr Crock.

'I think we will,' said the man. 'It won't take us long to pack up our things and be on our way.'

'But we'll tell the police,' said Emma. 'And you won't be able to use the

treasure to buy the meadow or build your rotten caravan park.'

'We never planned to build a caravan park,' said the man. 'It was just an excuse to dig for the treasure. And now we've got what we came for and nobody is going to stop us!'

'You can't leave us here,' said Emma.

'I can do anything I want,' laughed

the man. 'And it's no use calling for help either. Mr Brown has gone out for the day, and the other houses are too far away for anyone to hear.' The man gave a horrible, mocking laugh.

'Don't worry, Emma,' said Mr Crock. 'Your mum will come looking for us when you don't turn up at the cottage for lunch.'

'And we'll be long gone,' laughed the two men. They each took a handle of the heavy metal box, and carried the treasure chest away. Emma and Mr Crock watched as the two men hurried to pack up all their things.

'Oh dear,' sighed Emma. 'What are we going to do now?'

Then she had an idea. Sheltie. Of course. He must be hiding somewhere.

Sheltie would know what to do. She took in a deep breath and called out at the top of her voice.

'SHELTIE!'

Chapter Eleven

Sheltie wasn't very far away. He was in the next field behind a hedge. The little pony's ears pricked up as he heard Emma's voice.

Sheltie cocked his head to one side, listening. He trotted out into the middle of the lane.

Something was wrong. Where was Emma?

Sheltie looked around. His nostrils

flared as he sniffed at the air. Then he galloped over to the fence as fast as he could and stuck his head over the top rail.

Sheltie looked up and down the meadow. He couldn't see Emma anywhere but he could see the two men. And they were coming out of Prickly Thicket carrying the metal box.

'SHELTIE!' Emma called again.

This time Sheltie knew that Emma was in trouble and needed help.

Sheltie gave his head a good shake and blew a loud snort. Then, eyes bright and alert, he galloped up the lane back to the cottage.

When he got there the front gate was locked. The gate had been fitted with a

new safety bolt to stop Joshua running
out into the lane.

Sheltie looked at the bolt. It was just
like the special bolt on his paddock
gate. Sheltie saw the little pin which
held the bolt in place and carefully
pulled it free with his teeth. Then he
slipped the bolt across and pushed the

gate with his nose. Sheltie trotted round to the back of the cottage.

Police Constable Green's bicycle was propped up against the cottage wall. PC Green was inside collecting the posters Emma's mum had made.

Sheltie scraped at the kitchen door with his hoof. Emma's mum heard Sheltie outside and opened the door. Sheltie stamped his feet and pawed at the ground.

'What is it, Sheltie? Whatever's the matter?' said Mum. It was almost as if Sheltie was trying to tell her something. She stood at the open door and looked past the pony down the garden and into the empty paddock.

'Where's Emma?' said Mum. 'Is it Emma, Sheltie?'

Dad came out of the cottage with PC
Green.

'What's going on?' said the
policeman.

'It's Sheltie,' said Mum. 'He wants to
show us something. I think Emma's in
trouble.' She looked very worried. 'Go
on then, Sheltie. Show us!'

Sheltie gave a loud snort and trotted
off. He went a short way then stopped
and looked back.

'We're coming,' said the policeman.

Sheltie set off again looking back

from time to time to make sure that Mum and the policeman were following. Dad had stayed behind to look after Joshua and watched from the front gate as Sheltie led the way.

Chapter Twelve

The two men had finished loading their jeep. Major Armstrong's treasure chest sat between them on the front seat and the engine was running ready for their getaway.

The jeep rolled forward just as Sheltie burst through the gate into the meadow.

Sheltie ran straight at the jeep at a flat-out gallop. The man with the black beard was driving.

Suddenly Sheltie stopped, right in front of the moving jeep. The brave little pony stood his ground as the jeep roared towards him.

Emma and Mr Crock could see what was going on from Prickly Thicket. Emma gasped as she realized that Sheltie wasn't going to move out of the way.

At the last moment the jeep swerved to go around Sheltie. The sudden turn made the front wheels stick in one of the freshly dug holes and the jeep's engine stalled. Emma breathed a sigh of relief.

Sheltie turned and kicked out with his strong back legs. He kicked as hard as he could. His hooves hit the side of the jeep with a loud thud and made two big dents in the driver's door.

The other door of the jeep flew open and the man with red hair jumped out and tried to run away. PC Green brought him down with a flying tackle and knocked the air right out of him. The man lay on the grass, unable to move.

Sheltie stood guard over him,

stamping his hooves just in case he decided to run off again.

The driver had hit his head when the jeep stopped so suddenly. He sat forward in his seat, dizzy and dazed.

PC Green pulled the door open and reached inside the jeep. He took the jeep's keys and handcuffed the man to the steering wheel.

'Over here! We're over here!' called Emma.

PC Green called the station on his police radio while Mum ran over to the thicket. She found Emma and Mr Crock tied up beneath the tree. She quickly undid the ropes.

'I knew Sheltie would bring help,' said Emma. 'I just knew it!' She blurted out the whole story to Mum.

'We found the treasure. Major Armstrong's treasure, and now we can save Horseshoe Pond!'

Mum gave Emma a big hug. She was so pleased to find that Emma was safe.

A police Range Rover pulled up in the lane and three policemen took the two men to the police station. Emma ran up to Sheltie and threw her arms

around his neck. Sheltie's eyes twinkled and he gave a loud snort.

'Oh, Sheltie, you're so clever,' said Emma. Mr Crock and PC Green agreed.

'You always know just what to do!' said Emma.

Sheltie pawed at the ground with his hoof.

Back at the cottage PC Green opened the big metal chest. The lock was all rusty and the box had to be opened with one of Dad's drills and a pair of pliers. Inside the box were Major Armstrong's treasures. The valuables he had buried all those years ago.

There were silver candlesticks, twelve silver goblets, a set of silver spoons, two little gold statues and all

of Major Armstrong's war medals. And
in a big black velvet bag was the
family's collection of old gold coins.

'This lot must be worth a fortune,'
said the policeman. 'The Armstrongs
will be very pleased to hear about this!'

And indeed they were.

Up at Fox Hall Manor the family
were delighted to hear of Emma's find.
They offered a big reward.

As the treasure was found on Mr Brown's land, Emma and Mr Crock thought it was only right that the reward should go towards helping the farmer and saving Horseshoe Pond.

There was enough reward money to help Mr Brown without him having to sell off one piece of land. Horseshoe Pond was going to stay exactly as it was. Little Applewood would remain a peaceful little village. Thanks to Emma and Sheltie!

That evening Emma went out to the paddock with a bagful of fresh carrots. Sheltie was frisky, tossing his head and swishing his tail. When he saw Emma with the carrots he ran over and snatched the whole bag out of her hands. Then he ran off around the paddock, carrots spilling everywhere.

Emma laughed. 'Oh, Sheltie, you *are* naughty sometimes. But you're the best pony in the whole wide world!'

Sheltie munched the carrots and blew a raspberry. He had to agree. He *was* the smartest little pony ever.

If you like making friends, fun, excitement and adventure, then you'll love

The little pony with the big heart!

Sheltie is the lovable little Shetland pony with a big personality. He is cheeky, full of fun and has a heart of gold. His owner, Emma, knew that she and Sheltie would be best friends as soon as she saw him. She could tell that he thought so too by the way his brown eyes twinkled beneath his big, bushy mane. When Emma, her mum and dad and little brother, Joshua, first moved to Little Applewood, she thought that she might not like living there. But life is never dull with Sheltie around. He is full of mischief and he and Emma have lots of exciting adventures together.

Share Sheltie and Emma's adventures in:

SHELTIE THE SHETLAND PONY
SHELTIE AND THE RUNAWAY
SHELTIE FINDS A FRIEND
SHELTIE TO THE RESCUE
SHELTIE IN DANGER

READ MORE IN PUFFIN

For children of all ages, Puffin represents quality and variety – the very best in publishing today around the world.

For complete information about books available from Puffin – and Penguin – and how to order them, contact us at the appropriate address below. Please note that for copyright reasons the selection of books varies from country to country.

On the worldwide web: www.puffin.co.uk

In the United Kingdom: Please write to *Dept. EP, Penguin Books Ltd, Bath Road, Harmondsworth, West Drayton, Middlesex UB7 ODA*

In the United States: Please write to *Consumer Sales, Penguin USA, P.O. Box 999, Dept. 17109, Bergenfield, New Jersey 07621-0120*. VISA and MasterCard holders call 1-800-253-6476 to order Penguin titles

In Canada: Please write to *Penguin Books Canada Ltd, 10 Alcorn Avenue, Suite 300, Toronto, Ontario M4V 3B2*

In Australia: Please write to *Penguin Books Australia Ltd, P.O. Box 257, Ringwood, Victoria 3134*

In New Zealand: Please write to *Penguin Books (NZ) Ltd, Private Bag 102902, North Shore Mail Centre, Auckland 10*

In India: Please write to *Penguin Books India Pvt Ltd, 706 Eros Apartments, 56 Nehru Place, New Delhi 110 019*

In the Netherlands: Please write to *Penguin Books Netherlands bv, Postbus 3507, NL-1001 AH Amsterdam*

In Germany: Please write to *Penguin Books Deutschland GmbH, Metzlerstrasse 26, 60594 Frankfurt am Main*

In Spain: Please write to *Penguin Books S. A., Bravo Murillo 19, 1° B, 28015 Madrid*

In Italy: Please write to *Penguin Italia s.r.l., Via Felice Casati 20, I–20124 Milano*

In France: Please write to *Penguin France S. A., 17 rue Lejeune, F–31000 Toulouse*

In Japan: Please write to *Penguin Books Japan, Ishikiribashi Building, 2–5–4, Suido, Bunkyo-ku, Tokyo 112*

In South Africa: Please write to *Longman Penguin Southern Africa (Pty) Ltd, Private Bag X08, Bertsham 2013*

PUFFIN BOOKS

Sheltie Saves the Day

Make friends with

The little pony with the big heart

Sheltie is the lovable little Shetland pony with a big personality. He is cheeky, full of fun and has a heart of gold. His best friend and new owner is Emma, and together they have lots of exciting adventures.

Share Sheltie and Emma's adventures in

SHELTIE THE SHETLAND PONY
SHELTIE AND THE RUNAWAY
SHELTIE FINDS A FRIEND
SHELTIE TO THE RESCUE
SHELTIE IN DANGER

Peter Clover was born and went to school in London. He was a storyboard artist and illustrator before he began to put words to his pictures. He enjoys painting, travelling, cooking and keeping fit, and lives on the coast in Somerset.

Also by Peter Clover in Puffin

The Sheltie Series